BATAVIA PUBLIC LIBRARY DISTRICT
3 6173 00154 5154

P9-DID-186

A. Lincoln and Me

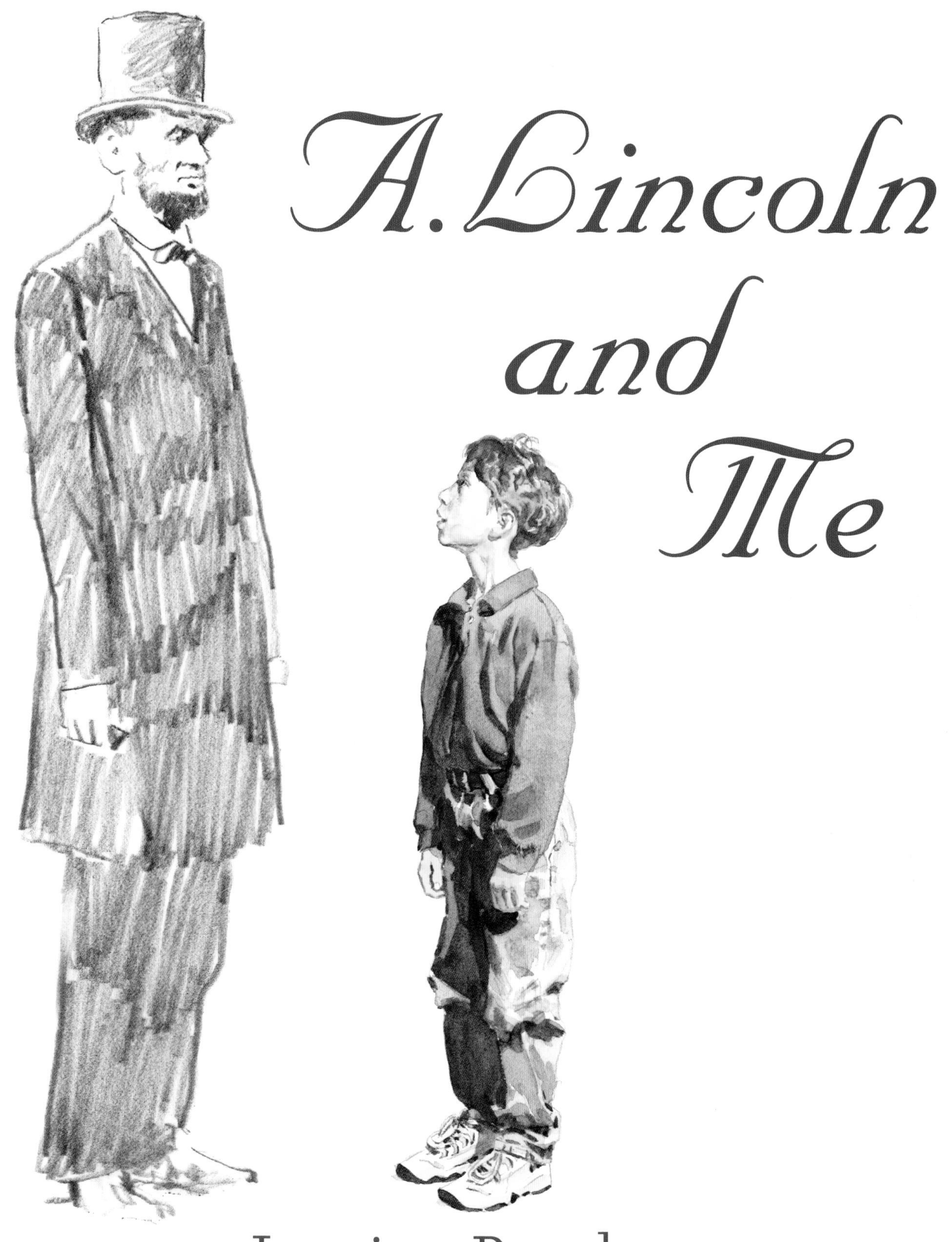

BY Louise Borden

ILLUSTRATED BY Ted Lewin

SCHOLASTIC PRESS • NEW YORK

For Pete, Catie, and Ayars,
and especially for Ted —L.B.

To Floyd and
Stella Dickman —T.L.

SPECIAL THANKS TO THE CINCINNATI HISTORICAL SOCIETY.

LIBRARY OF CONGRESS CATALOG NUMBER: 98-51921
ISBN 0-590-45714-4

10 9 8 7 6 5 4 3 2 1 9/9 0/0 01 02 03 04

Printed in Hong Kong 38
First edition, October 1999

The illustrations in this book were painted in watercolors. The display type was set in Nuptial Script. The text type was set in Joanna.
Book design by Marijka Kostiw

There are 365 birthdays,
one for every day of the year,
and I have the same one as Abraham Lincoln.
February 12th.
A day of winter
when we both were born.

When February comes,
we talk about Abraham Lincoln in class.
My teacher, Mrs. Giff, hangs 28 pictures of Lincoln along the hall.
We'll all remember him when we get a day off from school.

Mrs. Giff says we're a lot alike,
old Abraham Lincoln and me.
She says I'm as skinny as a beanpole
and tall for my age.
Just like Abraham was
when he started reading books.

Sometimes I have big, clumsy hands.
And big, clumsy feet.
I never see WET PAINT
until it's too late.

"Big Butterfingers!" yells Holly
in her extra-loud voice.
"Big Butterfeet!" yells Carlos
and he runs to tell my friends.

“Big hands,” I say,
and I look down at mine.

“Lincoln had big hands, too.
Strong hands,” says my teacher.
“Strong enough to split rails for a fence,
and wrestle two men at a time,
and pull 36 states back together.”

I think about all those different states,
like pieces in a puzzle.
Some joining north,
and some joining south.
States where everyone was free.
States where some folks were not.

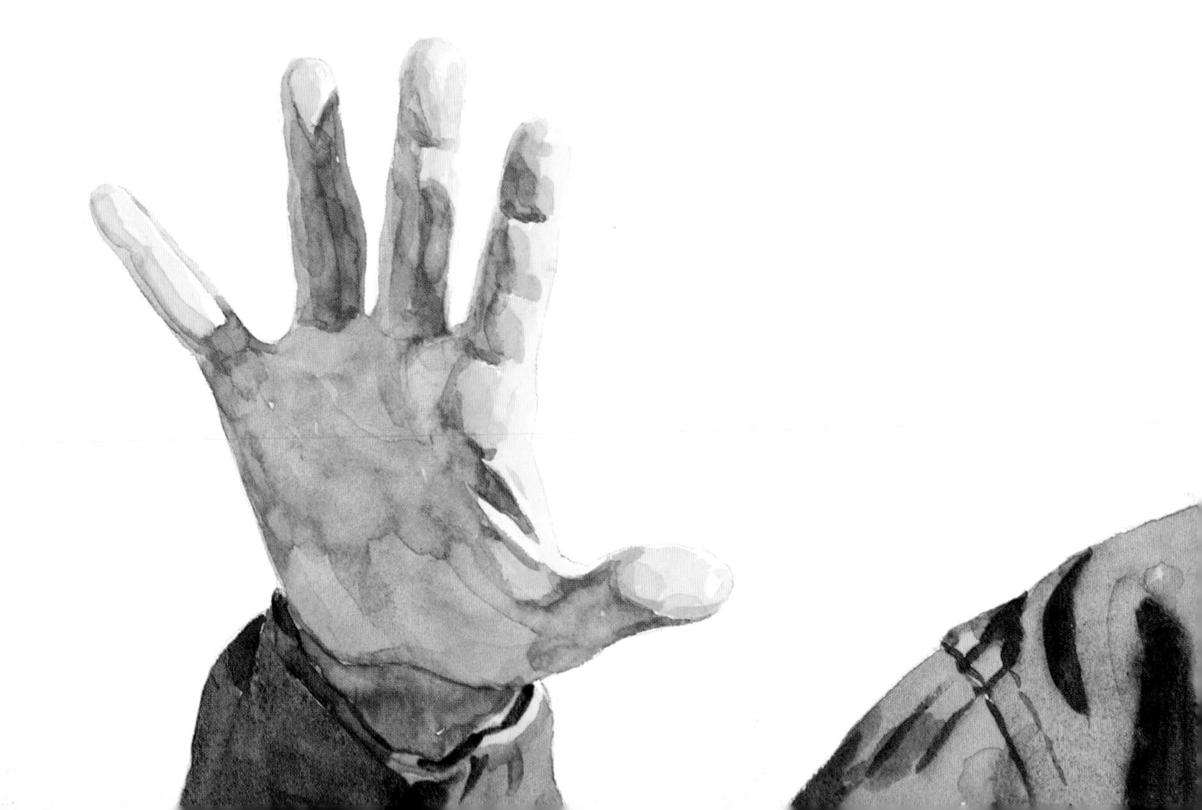

"Big hands and a big heart," says Mrs. Giff
as we mop up the mess.

Later I hear her tell James and Trish:
"Half a nation once called Lincoln many names . . .
like gorilla
and baboon
and backwoods hick."

At recess, Mrs. Giff tells us that people laughed
at Lincoln's frontier ways . . .
at his hair that wouldn't comb . . .
at his long, lanky legs.
People figured
he wouldn't know how to be President
if he didn't have fancy manners,
if he'd been poor, growing up.

Abraham Lincoln has his very own shelf in our school library.
There's a lot to say about this man
who had big hands
and big feet.
Who was tall for his age,
just like me.

For starters,
he didn't like to be called Abe.
So I call him A. Lincoln,
the same as his signature
in all those books.

There is A. Lincoln,
when I'm not even looking . . .
on the shiny pennies
that jingle in my pocket.

He doesn't look like someone who walked barefoot to school.
He doesn't look like someone whose mother couldn't write or read.
He just looks like himself.

He's on pennies today
because he's a hero.
Because he talked in words
that people could understand.
Because he told all the slaves,
"Now you are free."

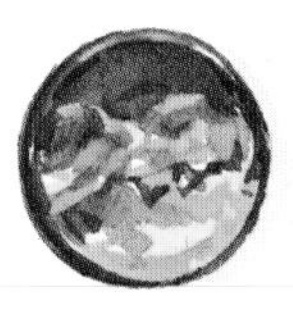

IN GOD

I think about Lincoln
when I'm the line leader at school.

I think about Lincoln
when I'm reading good books
and I don't want them to end.

I think about Lincoln
when I'm singing in the back row,
a head above my friends.

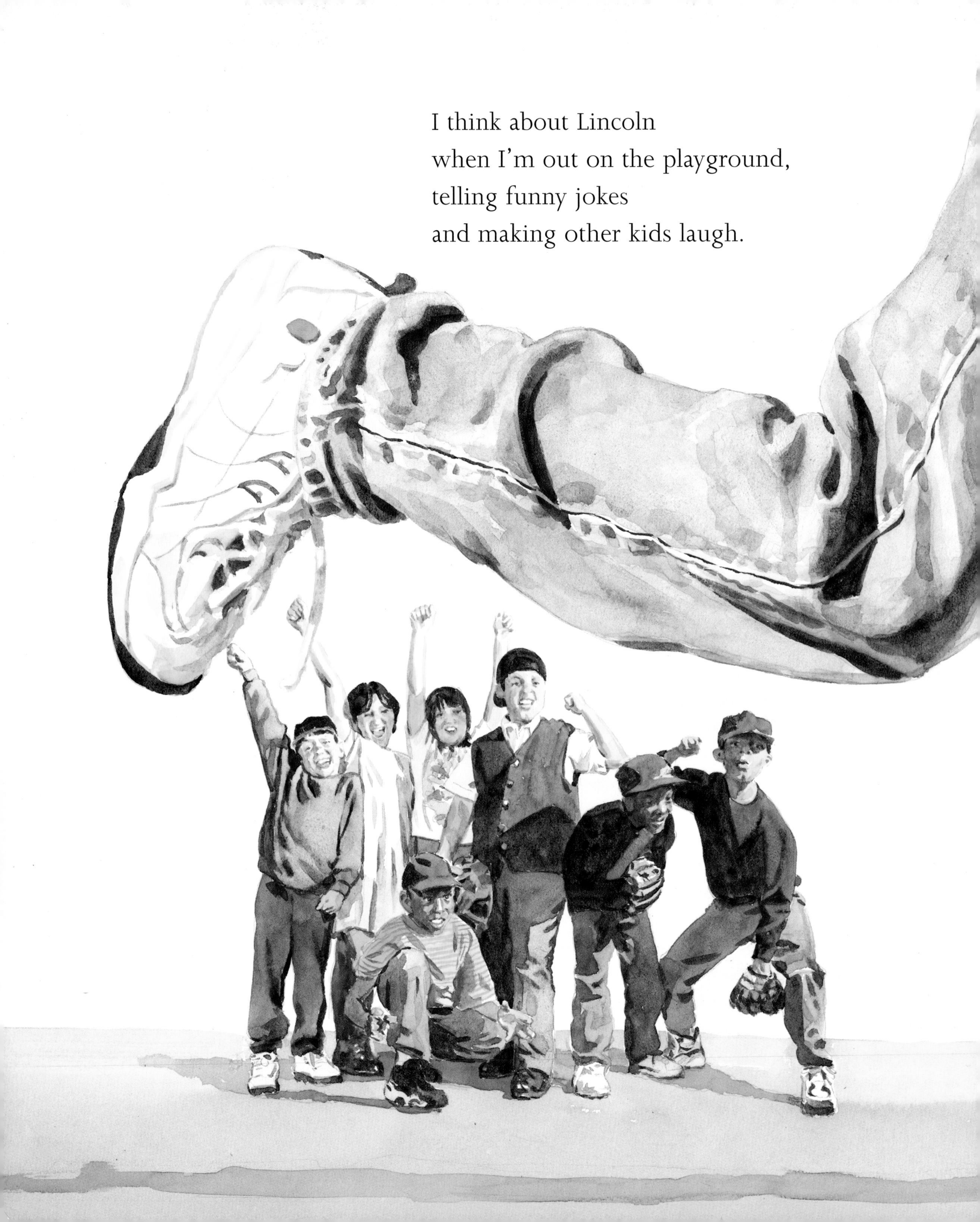

I think about Lincoln
when I'm out on the playground,
telling funny jokes
and making other kids laugh.

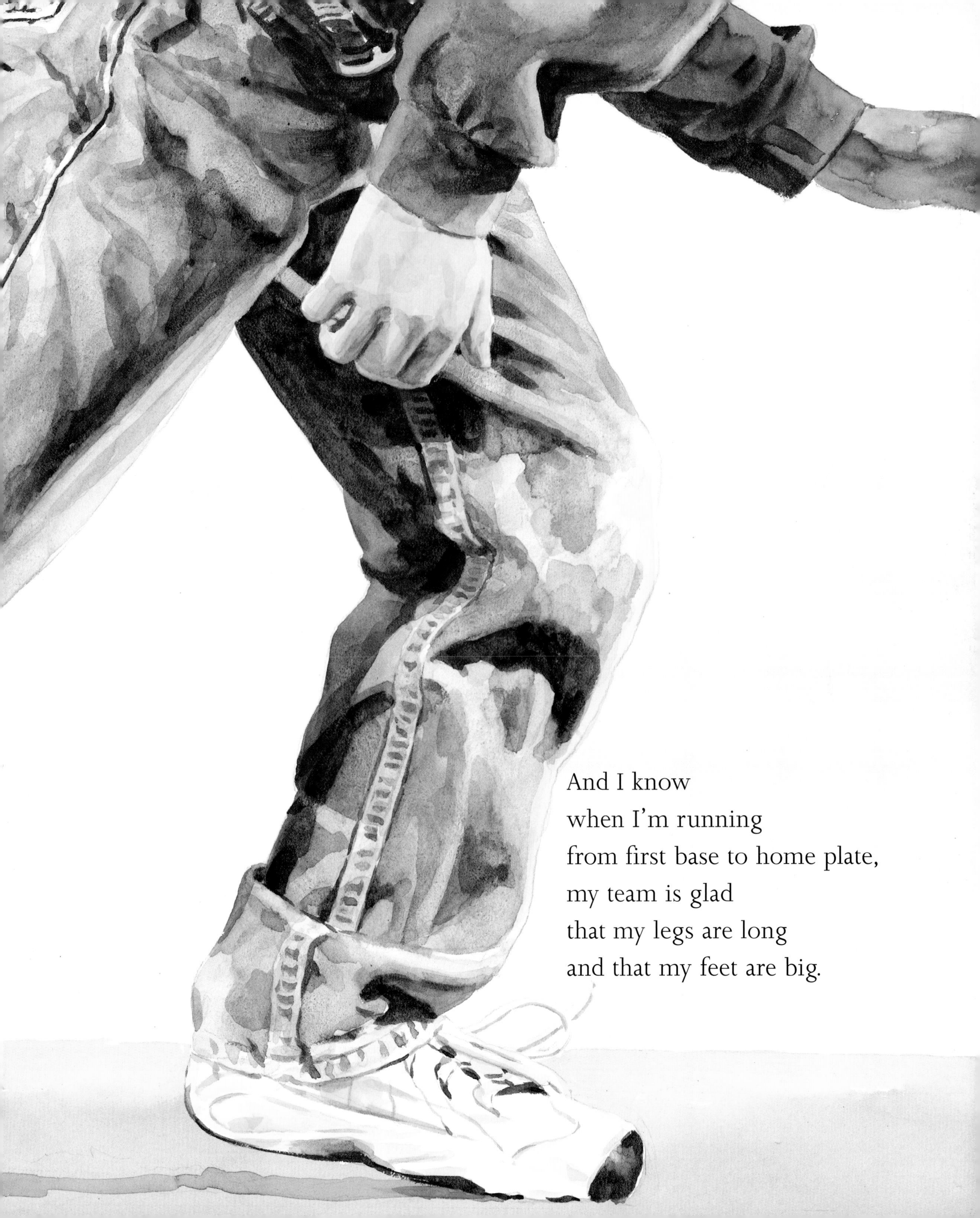

And I know
when I'm running
from first base to home plate,
my team is glad
that my legs are long
and that my feet are big.

On the way home from school,
I see A. Lincoln,
standing tall and bronze in the afternoon sun.
Big buttons on his coat.
Big words in his heart.
Big hands and big feet
like mine.

But I wasn't born in the backwoods of Kentucky.
And my house in the city doesn't have a dirt floor.
It has a lot of windows.
A. Lincoln's log cabin only had one.

When I do my homework,
I borrow some chalk
from my brother, Sam.
Then I write out numbers
on the back of a shovel,
the way A. Lincoln did arithmetic,
long ago.

"Listen,
nobody can be another Abraham Lincoln."
That's what my brother, Sam, says
when I tape Lincoln's signature
just above my bed.

But his birthday's mine, too,
marked on calendars for all to see:
February 12th,
a day of winter,
to celebrate Lincoln and me.

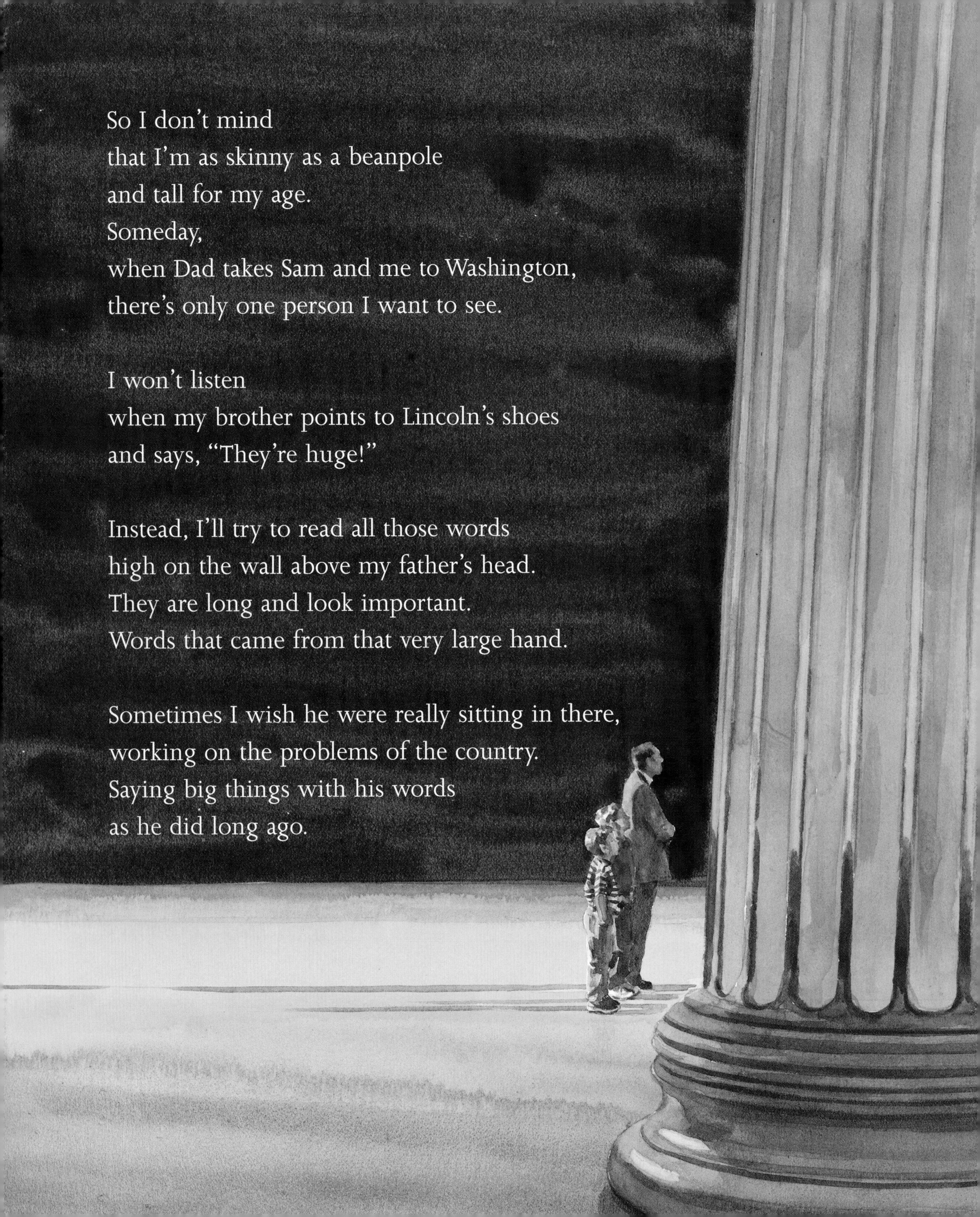

So I don't mind
that I'm as skinny as a beanpole
and tall for my age.
Someday,
when Dad takes Sam and me to Washington,
there's only one person I want to see.

I won't listen
when my brother points to Lincoln's shoes
and says, "They're huge!"

Instead, I'll try to read all those words
high on the wall above my father's head.
They are long and look important.
Words that came from that very large hand.

Sometimes I wish he were really sitting in there,
working on the problems of the country.
Saying big things with his words
as he did long ago.

My brother, Sam, is right about one thing:
nobody can be another Abraham Lincoln.
But then, I figure,
nobody can be another me.